THE BOXCAR CHILDREN
SURPRISE ISLAND
THE YELLOW HOUSE MYSTERY
MYSTERY RANCH
MIKE'S MYSTERY
BLUE BAY MYSTERY
THE WOODSHED MYSTERY
THE LIGHTHOUSE MYSTERY
MOUNTAIN TOP MYSTERY
SCHOOLHOUSE MYSTERY
CABOOSE MYSTERY
HOUSEBOAT MYSTERY
SNOWBOUND MYSTERY
TREE HOUSE MYSTERY
BICYCLE MYSTERY
MYSTERY IN THE SAND
MYSTERY BEHIND THE WALL
BUS STATION MYSTERY
BENNY UNCOVERS A MYSTERY
THE HAUNTED CABIN MYSTERY
THE DESERTED LIBRARY MYSTERY
THE ANIMAL SHELTER MYSTERY
THE OLD MOTEL MYSTERY
THE MYSTERY OF THE HIDDEN
   PAINTING
THE AMUSEMENT PARK MYSTERY
THE MYSTERY OF THE MIXED-UP ZOO
THE CAMP-OUT MYSTERY
THE MYSTERY GIRL
THE MYSTERY CRUISE
THE DISAPPEARING FRIEND MYSTERY
THE MYSTERY OF THE SINGING GHOST
MYSTERY IN THE SNOW
THE PIZZA MYSTERY
THE MYSTERY HORSE
THE MYSTERY AT THE DOG SHOW
THE CASTLE MYSTERY
THE MYSTERY OF THE LOST VILLAGE
THE MYSTERY ON THE ICE
THE MYSTERY OF THE PURPLE POOL
THE GHOST SHIP MYSTERY

THE MYSTERY IN WASHINGTON, DC
THE CANOE TRIP MYSTERY
THE MYSTERY OF THE HIDDEN BEACH
THE MYSTERY OF THE MISSING CAT
THE MYSTERY AT SNOWFLAKE INN
THE MYSTERY ON STAGE
THE DINOSAUR MYSTERY
THE MYSTERY OF THE STOLEN MUSIC
THE MYSTERY AT THE BALL PARK
THE CHOCOLATE SUNDAE MYSTERY
THE MYSTERY OF THE HOT
   AIR BALLOON
THE MYSTERY BOOKSTORE
THE PILGRIM VILLAGE MYSTERY
THE MYSTERY OF THE STOLEN
   BOXCAR
THE MYSTERY IN THE CAVE
THE MYSTERY ON THE TRAIN
THE MYSTERY AT THE FAIR
THE MYSTERY OF THE LOST MINE
THE GUIDE DOG MYSTERY
THE HURRICANE MYSTERY
THE PET SHOP MYSTERY
THE MYSTERY OF THE SECRET MESSAGE
THE FIREHOUSE MYSTERY
THE MYSTERY IN SAN FRANCISCO
THE NIAGARA FALLS MYSTERY
THE MYSTERY AT THE ALAMO
THE OUTER SPACE MYSTERY
THE SOCCER MYSTERY
THE MYSTERY IN THE OLD ATTIC
THE GROWLING BEAR MYSTERY
THE MYSTERY OF THE LAKE MONSTER
THE MYSTERY AT PEACOCK HALL
THE WINDY CITY MYSTERY
THE BLACK PEARL MYSTERY
THE CEREAL BOX MYSTERY
THE PANTHER MYSTERY
THE MYSTERY OF THE QUEEN'S JEWELS
THE STOLEN SWORD MYSTERY
THE BASKETBALL MYSTERY

THE VAMPIRE MYSTERY

created by

GERTRUDE CHANDLER WARNER

Illustrated by Robert Papp

ALBERT WHITMAN & Company
Chicago, Illinois

Library of Congress Cataloging-in-Publication Data

Warner, Gertrude Chandler.
The vampire mystery / created by Gertrude Chandler Warner ; illustrated by
Robert Papp.
p. cm. — (The Boxcar children mysteries ; 120)
Summary: When the Aldens agree to watch the house of a local author who
has written a book about a vampire, they end up investigating activities that
are suspiciously similar to those in his book.
ISBN 978-0-8075-8460-6 (hardcover)
ISBN 978-0-8075-8461-3 (pbk.)
[1. Vampires—Fiction. 2. Brothers and sisters—Fiction. 3. Orphans—Fiction.
4. Mystery and detective stories.] I. Papp, Robert, ill. II. Title.
PZ7.W244Vam 2009
[Fic]—dc22
2009018564

10 9 8 7 6 5 4 LB 15 14 13 12 11

Cover art by Robert Papp.

For information about Albert Whitman & Company,
visit our web site at www.albertwhitman.com.

Contents

Contents

THE VAMPIRE MYSTERY

CHAPTER 1

The Greenfield Vampire

"Just this one book please," six-year-old Benny said. He gave *The Legend of the Vampire* to the librarian. On the cover was a picture of a scary man in a dark cape. He had two sharp teeth and blood red lips.

"Oh, Benny, are you sure that is a good book for you?" asked twelve-year-old Jessie. She was twelve and kept an eye on her younger brother. "I could help you pick out another."

"No, I want this one, Jessie," Benny said.

"Henry found it in the local author's section."

"It was written by Mr. Charles Hudson," explained Henry. At fourteen, he was the oldest.

"Oh!" exclaimed ten-year-old Violet. "Is that the author Grandfather told us about this morning?"

"I think it is," Henry said.

Mrs. Skylar, the librarian, smiled at the four Alden children. "Mr. Hudson is a local author who has written many exciting books. *The Legend of the Vampire* is one of his best selling stories. It's set right here in Greenfield."

Violet shivered. "A vampire in Greenfield?" she asked.

"Vampires aren't real, Violet," Jessie said. She put her arm around her sister's shoulders.

"Are you sure?" asked Benny.

"We're sure," Henry said. "Vampires are not real. They're just part of scary stories that people like to read for fun."

"Not real—like ghosts and monsters under your bed?" asked Benny.

"Yes, exactly like that," Jessie said.

"I like scary stories," Benny said. "They always have mysteries in them!" He opened the book to the first page. "'The cem... cem...'" Benny was just learning how to read.

"Cemetery," Henry helped.

"'The cemetery on...'" Benny scratched his forehead.

Violet looked over his shoulder at the page. "Whittaker Street," she told her little brother.

"'Was...dark...and...'" Benny sounded out the words. He sighed. "It's too hard for me. Can you read it to me, Henry?"

"Sure, Benny," Henry said. "But it's getting late now. We promised to meet Grandfather at eleven o'clock."

Jessie looked at her watch. "You're right, Henry." She handed her library card to Mrs. Skylar and checked out her novel. "Grandfather said that he wanted us to meet an old friend of his."

"Do you have the address where Grandfather wants to meet us?" Violet asked.

Henry patted his pocket. "Yes, I have it," he said. "I don't think it's very far. It's on the east end of town."

"Will we be passing any places to eat on the way?" Benny asked hopefully.

"Oh, Benny!" Jessie laughed. Benny had a big appetite. "How can you possibly be hungry after all those pancakes Mrs. McGregor made for you this morning?"

Mrs. McGregor was the Alden's housekeeper. She was a wonderful cook as well.

Benny patted his growling stomach. "I don't know, Jessie," he said. "I guess that's one mystery I'll never be able to solve!"

The Alden children laughed and hopped on their bikes. In ten minutes they found 52 Whittaker Street. It was an old, quaint house with a small lawn and a blooming flower garden. Grandfather's car was parked out front. He stood on the pale lavender porch talking to a tall man with white hair and a white mustache.

"What a beautiful house!" Violet exclaimed. She was wearing a pale purple top that matched the color of the porch almost exactly. It was her favorite color.

"Why, thank you," the man said, smiling at Violet.

Grandfather rested his hand on Benny's shoulder. "Mr. Hudson, I would like to introduce you to my family. This is Henry, Jessie, Violet, and Benny."

After their parents died, the Alden children ran away. They lived in an abandoned boxcar in the woods until their grandfather found them. He brought them to live with him in his big, white house in Greenfield.

"We're very pleased to meet you," Jessie said.

"Mr. Hudson?" Violet's face flushed red. "The famous author?"

Mr. Hudson laughed. "I'm not all that famous, you know," he said.

"You *are* famous!" Benny cried. He pulled *The Legend of the Vampire* from his backpack. "Your book was in the library!"

Just then a big, blue car screeched to a halt in front of the house. A young man in a business suit jumped out. He hurried up the sidewalk.

"This is the last time!" he said. He hammered a "For Sale" sign into the lawn. His face was red.

Grandfather looked puzzled.

"Don't mind Josh," Mr. Hudson said. "He is my realtor and someone keeps stealing his sign from my front lawn. He's been quite upset by it."

Benny looked at Josh banging away on the metal sign. "What's a realtor?" he asked.

"A realtor is a person who tries to help you sell your home," Jessie explained.

"Let me give Josh a hand." Grandfather went over and held the sign steady while Josh hammered.

"Are you moving away from Greenfield, Mr. Hudson?" Henry asked.

"No. I love Greenfield," Mr. Hudson said. "I don't really even want to sell my home." He sighed and looked up at the pretty house. "I've lived here all my life, but it is too big of a place for one old man to take care of on his own. When the house is sold, I'll move to an apartment on the other side of town."

"You mean *if* the house is ever sold," Josh said, wiping his forehead.

"Now, Josh," Mr. Hudson scolded. "Just because the sign keeps disappearing doesn't mean we can't sell the house."

"No, but the broken flowerpots and the old cemetery out back don't help either."

"Old cemetery?" asked Violet.

"Yes," Mr. Hudson replied. "It's quite historic. Some of Greenfield's first citizens are buried back there. You kids are welcome to go take a look. It's actually very beautiful and peaceful."

"Except when the vampire is prowling," Josh added.

The Aldens were too surprised to speak. Violet's face turned white.

"Don't pay attention to Josh," Mr. Hudson hurriedly said. "He gets overly excited sometimes. The vampire is just an old legend."

"But, you said you saw..." Josh tried to argue.

"Now is not the time or place to discuss this, Josh," Mr. Hudson said, glancing over at the Aldens.

"Let's take a walk out back," Jessie said to her sister and brothers. Benny held tightly to Jessie's hand, and Violet stayed close to Henry's side as the Aldens walked back to see the old cemetery. The grass was neatly cut between the rows of the weather-worn headstones.

"What's a legend, anyway?" asked Benny as the children walked.

"It's an old story that has become famous," Jessie said.

"Like Paul Bunyan and his big blue ox," Henry said. "That story is a legend."

Just then the Aldens heard a loud sound in the quiet cemetery. They stopped walking and stared at each other.

Benny groaned. "I'm sorry. I can't help it," he said. "I'm so hungry my stomach keeps growling."

Henry laughed. "I think your appetite is becoming a legend, Benny."

"I know," Benny said. "Right now I think I could eat more than both Paul Bunyan and his ox!"

Violet bent over to look at an old headstone with a pretty flower carved on its front. "This one is hundreds of years old," she said. "The person buried here died in 1742." As she stood up, something caught her eye at the edge of the cemetery.

"Look!" Violet gripped Henry's arm. "There's someone staring at us over there!"

Henry, Jessie, and Benny turned just in time to see the man. He wore a long, dark coat. When he saw that the children had spotted him, he ducked behind a tree and disappeared into the woods.

Violet shivered. "That was odd," she said.

"Not really, Violet," said Henry. "Maybe he was just taking a walk, the same as we were."

"I'm sure Henry's right," Jessie said. "But let's get back to Grandfather now."

CHAPTER 2

An Offer to Help

"What do you think of our little cemetery?" Mr. Hudson asked as the children stepped back onto the porch.

"It is quiet and peaceful," Jessie said. "Just like you said it would be."

Josh was rocking back and forth on a squeaky wooden rocking chair in the corner. He glanced at Jessie then quickly looked away and bit down on his lower lip.

"I sure hope you will all stay for some lunch," said Mr. Hudson.

"Lunch? You bet!" cried Benny. "What are we having?"

"Oh, Benny, that's not polite," Jessie said.

"I'm sorry, Mr. Hudson. I didn't mean to be rude." Benny sniffed the air. "But I can smell something really good."

Mr. Hudson laughed. "It tastes as good as it smells, Benny. That's my famous red clam chowder cooking on the stove. I made a big pot of it and I have a plate of sandwiches as well."

"Clam chowder!" Benny said. "That's my favorite!"

Jessie and Benny set the table, and Henry and Violet poured tall glasses of lemonade for everyone. The kitchen had wide oak floors and pretty flowered curtains on the windows.

"Your home is so beautiful, Mr. Hudson," Violet said.

"Thank you, Violet." Mr. Hudson filled her bowl with hot soup. "I do hate to sell it. It is filled with so many memories. My parents moved here years ago before I was even born. They hoped that the house would always stay in our family."

"Did you write all your books here, Mr. Hudson?" asked Henry. He took a turkey sandwich and passed the tray to Grandfather.

"Yes, Henry, I did. There's a small room upstairs that looks out over the cemetery and the woods. I started writing stories up there when I was a little boy. I get some of my best ideas when I am looking out that window."

Josh dropped his spoon. "Is that where you were when you saw the vampire?" he said.

Mr. Hudson shook his head. "Now, Josh, I thought we agreed not to talk about such things."

"You agreed. I did not." Josh pushed his chair back from the table. "Until we solve this vampire problem, I don't see how I will be able to sell this house. Mrs. Fairfax says she found blood on her back porch yesterday! Some of the other neighbors have heard strange sounds coming from the cemetery at night. Word is getting around town that the vampire in your book has come to life."

The Alden children looked at each other

across the table. Benny sat very still, the soup spoon frozen at his lips.

"Josh, please stop that vampire talk. You know it is just a story," Mr. Hudson said.

Josh shrugged. "I'm only trying to do my job."

Mr. Hudson shook his head. "I don't think this kind of talk is helping."

Josh stood abruptly. "I'm sorry, but I have to get back to the office, now. Thanks for the lunch, Charles. Call me before you leave," he added. The screen door slammed behind him.

Mr. Hudson sighed. "Josh is so excitable," he said. "I should have hired a nice, calm realtor to sell my house."

"Is there really a vampire around here?" Benny asked.

"Of course not," Grandfather answered. "Vampires are not real."

"Your grandfather is right," Mr. Hudson said. "When I was growing up in this house, there was an old legend about a vampire around here. People said prowled the town at night and brought his victims to the cemetery. During the daytime, he hid in his coffin and slept. I always loved scary stories. As a matter of fact, I used to frighten my little brother by telling him all about the vampire. Sometimes, he was so afraid that he would have to sleep in my bed with me. I thought that the vampire story was so much fun that when I grew up I turned it into a book."

"*The Legend of the Vampire*!" Benny cried. "We checked it out of the library this morning. It's outside in my backpack."

"Yes, Benny. That's the one. It became a popular book. It has been so popular that I am hoping to convince a producer to turn my book into a movie."

"How exciting," said Jessie. "Would it be filmed here in Greenfield?"

Mr. Hudson refilled Benny's bowl with chowder. "I had hoped so," Mr. Hudson said. "I was supposed to go out of town to meet with some people to discuss the project. But with the house for sale, I'm not sure that I can leave just now. There's no one to look after the place while I'm away."

"We would be happy to do it," Henry offered.

"Yes," Jessie added. "We could check on it every day if you like."

"Are you sure?" Mr. Hudson asked. "You really wouldn't mind? I would be happy to pay you."

"We're sure," Violet said. "And you don't have to pay us anything. We can ride our bikes over. I'll water the flowers out front in the garden."

"And I can cut the lawn," Henry said.

"Benny and I will sweep the porch and dust the furniture for you," Jessie said.

Grandfather smiled. "My grandchildren are very helpful."

"I can see that," Mr. Hudson said. "And I'm very grateful. Now I can go away without worrying that I might lose a sale because the house is not in good shape."

After Grandfather left to attend a business meeting, Mr. Hudson walked with the Aldens to the back of the house. He opened the door to the shed. "The lawn mower is a little old," he said to Henry. "Sometimes it acts up."

"Don't worry, Mr. Hudson," Jessie said. "Henry is very good with motors and with fixing things."

The shed was large, but dark. Mr. Hudson called the children over to the corner. He lifted a clay flowerpot from a wooden shelf. "This is where I keep a spare key to the house," he said. "It will be right here under this pot whenever you need to get inside."

"Wow, this is a cool bike," Violet said, running her hand over the shiny front fender of an old-fashioned blue bicycle.

Violet admiring old bicycle.

"Yes," said Mr. Hudson. "It is very old, but I like to keep it in good shape. It belongs to my brother. It's odd, though. I thought that I had stored the bicycle in the back of the shed. I wonder how it got up here?"

"Does your brother live nearby?" asked Benny.

Mr. Hudson dropped his hands into his pockets. He looked at the ground for a few moments before answering. "No. I'm sorry

to say that my brother and I had a fight a long time ago when we were younger. My brother left town and I never heard from him again. It was a silly fight. I don't even remember what it was about anymore. It happened over forty years ago."

Suddenly, everyone heard loud shouts coming from the front of the house. They ran from the shed. An older woman was pointing at the Aldens' bicycles and calling out for Mr. Hudson.

"Look at this!" she cried. "Bicycles are blocking the sidewalk! How am I supposed to get my shopping cart past? I think I hurt my ankle on this one." Mrs. Fairfax pointed at Benny's small bike.

"Hold on, Martha," Mr. Hudson said. "We'll get them out of your way."

Henry, Jessie, Violet, and Benny quickly moved their bicycles onto the lawn. Mrs. Fairfax glared at them.

"We're so sorry," Jessie said. "It was careless of us to leave our bikes there. We hope your ankle doesn't hurt too badly."

"Children are always careless!" Mrs. Fairfax said. "These children aren't moving in here, are they, Charles?" she asked.

"These are the Aldens," Mr. Hudson said. "They are the grandchildren of James Alden, an old friend of mine. They will be looking after my house while I am away on business."

Mrs. Fairfax pushed her glasses up on her nose and stared at each of the Aldens. "Well, you better make sure they don't leave their things lying around in my way."

"We won't do that, Mrs. Fairfax," Henry promised.

Mrs. Fairfax marched up the sidewalk and into her home.

Mr. Hudson sighed. "I'm sorry about that, children," he said. "Mrs. Fairfax is not a bad lady. She was a good friend of my brother's and has lived next door to me for fifty years. But she is worried that I might sell my home to a noisy family with lots of children and barking dogs. She likes her peace and quiet."

"We'll park our bikes behind the house from now on," Henry said. "We should never have left them on the sidewalk."

The four Aldens said goodbye to Mr. Hudson. As they pedaled toward home, they saw Mrs. Fairfax staring at them from the front window of her house.

CHAPTER 3

A Missing Book

After dinner, the Aldens each took a slice of Mrs. McGregor's apple pie and headed outside to the front porch. Watch, their wire-haired terrier, raced outdoors with them.

"How did the smallest Alden end up with the biggest piece of pie?" asked Henry.

Benny, his cheeks stuffed with the delicious dessert, shrugged his shoulders.

"Henry," asked Violet, "what do you really think about the vampire story? It seems like Mr. Hudson did see something in the cemetery that scared him."

"I'm sure the vampire's not real, Violet. But something odd does seem to be going on at Mr. Hudson's house."

"Yes," said Jessie. "Why would someone steal the 'For Sale' sign on his front lawn?"

"I'm not sure," said Henry. "Maybe it was just a joke."

Violet shook her head. "Josh certainly wasn't laughing."

"No," Jessie replied. "And Josh seemed really upset by the vampire story. I wish we knew a little more about that legend. It might help us to solve the mystery of what is going on at Mr. Hudson's house."

Benny jumped from his chair and dashed into the house. He returned with his backpack. Watch barked excitedly.

"Benny, what are you doing?" asked Jessie.

"It's a clue!" Benny replied. "The book I got at the library yesterday that Mr. Hudson wrote. I put it in my backpack."

"That's right, Benny!" Henry said. "I had forgotten about *The Legend of the Vampire*."

"And didn't Mr. Hudson say that he based his book on the old vampire legend?" asked Violet.

"Yes, he did," said Jessie. "Good work, Benny."

Benny reached into his backpack. A funny look came over his face.

"What's wrong?" asked Jessie.

"I know I put the book in my backpack," he said. "But now it's not here."

"Maybe you took it out when you got home," suggested Violet.

"No, I'm sure I didn't," Benny said.

"Could it have fallen out?" asked Jessie.

"I don't think so," Benny said. "There are no holes in my backpack. But maybe I didn't zip it closed all the way."

"We should ride our bikes back to the library and to Mr. Hudson's," Henry suggested. "We can look along the streets to check if the book fell out."

Henry, Jessie, Violet, and Benny strapped on their helmets and rode to the library. It was almost closing time.

"Hello, children," said Mrs. Skylar. "The library will be closing in about ten minutes. Can I help you find something?"

"No, thank you, Mrs. Skylar," said Henry. "We were wondering if anyone turned in *The Legend of the Vampire*."

Mrs. Skylar went to her computer and clicked the keys. "No," she said. "The computer shows that it was checked out this morning by Benny. Did something happen to the book?"

"We seem to have misplaced it," said Jessie. "But I'm sure we'll find it soon."

"I hope so," said Mrs. Skylar. "Good luck."

"Don't look so sad, Benny," said Jessie. "We still might find the book outside Mr. Hudson's house."

The four Aldens rode quickly through Greenfield until they arrived at Whittaker Street. It was still light out, but the sun was beginning to set behind Mr. Hudson's house.

The woods and the cemetery were full of shadows.

Henry, Jessie, Violet, and Benny spread out and searched the sidewalk and the lawn. There was no sign of the book.

"Maybe Mr. Hudson found it already," Violet suggested. "He might have the book inside."

Henry knocked on the door, but no one answered. It was very quiet.

Suddenly, a loud clatter came from the side yard. The children ran to the edge of the porch. Their bicycles were lying in a heap on the ground.

"That's odd," said Henry.

"Maybe it was the wind," Violet suggested.

Benny jumped over the porch rail and picked up his bike. "It's not very windy." Something caught his eye and he pointed toward the cemetery. "Look!"

"What do you see?" asked Jessie.

But whatever it was, it was gone.

"I don't know," Benny said. "I thought I saw someone in a dark cape running. But I

guess it was just a shadow."

"We should get home," Henry said. "Grandfather doesn't like us riding our bikes in the dark. And it is getting late."

"But what about the book?" asked Benny. "We still haven't found it."

"Don't worry," said Jessie. "If we don't find it by the due date, we'll all chip in from our allowance money to pay for the book."

"Hey! Is that you Alden children over there making all that clatter?" Mrs. Fairfax was leaning against the rail of her front porch.

"We're sorry," Henry called. "The wind knocked our bicycles over. We're leaving now."

"I hope so," she said, turning away and stomping back toward her front door. "A person can't get any peace around here. And stop running through my backyard!"

"But we…" Violet wanted to explain that they had not run through her yard, but Mrs. Fairfax was already inside, the screen door slamming shut behind her.

"Why is she so angry?" asked Benny.

"Mrs. Fairfax probably just likes her peace and quiet," Violet said. "I suppose she's not used to such noises on this street. Maybe we frightened her."

"I hope I don't upset her when I have to cut the lawn," Henry added. "Lawn mowers make plenty of noise."

"So does my stomach," said Benny. "All this bike riding has made me hungry."

Henry laughed. "Let's go home and get you another piece of Mrs. McGregor's pie."

CHAPTER 4

Lost!

The next morning Mrs. McGregor placed a large platter of steaming waffles on the breakfast table.

"Here you go, Benny," she said. "I made a special waffle for you."

Benny had been sitting with his head in his hands. He looked up to see what Mrs. McGregor had made. It was a large round waffle with strawberries for eyes and a blueberry mouth. Fluffy white whipped cream hair sat on top.

"Wow! Thank you, Mrs. McGregor." Benny grabbed his fork.

"There's the smile we like to see," said Grandfather. "Are you feeling better now?"

Benny's mouth was stuffed full with waffle and fruit.

Jessie answered for him. "Benny's not sick, Grandfather. He feels badly because he can't find *The Legend of the Vampire*, the book he checked out of the library yesterday."

"Perhaps it's in your room, Benny," Grandfather suggested.

Benny shook his head.

Violet spooned fruit over her waffle. "We searched everywhere," she said.

"It was in his backpack when we were at Mr. Hudson's house. By the time we got home, it had mysteriously disappeared. We even checked at the library to see if anyone had turned it in." Henry poured himself a glass of orange juice.

"That *is* a mystery," Grandfather said. "But I'm sure you children will figure it out."

The Aldens loved mysteries and they had already solved quite a few since coming to live with Grandfather.

"Maybe you can check at the library again today," Grandfather said. "They are having their annual fair and bake sale on the front lawn. It might be fun to stop by."

A timer in the kitchen rang. "That must be my pie," Mrs. McGregor said, wiping her hands on her apron. "I made an apple pie and a lemon cake to donate to the bake sale. If you children want, you can come with me this morning when I drop them off at the library."

"That reminds me," Grandfather said. "Mr. Hudson called this morning. He will be leaving on his business trip shortly. He asked if you children could stop by the house later today to cut the lawn and make sure everything is neat and in order. A young couple from out of town will be stopping by to look at the house this afternoon. Mr. Hudson is hoping that they will be interested in buying it."

"Are you sure Mr. Hudson called this morning?" asked Henry. "We thought he might have left for his trip last night."

"No," Grandfather said. "It was this morning. He said he was packing his bags as he spoke to me."

"We'll go to Mr. Hudson's after the library," Henry said.

"It's such a beautiful house," Violet added. "We'll make sure it is in good shape when that couple arrives. I'm sure they'll love it."

Henry, Jessie, Violet, and Benny helped Mrs. McGregor with the dishes and then carefully placed the baked goods in the car.

"The car smells so good!" Benny exclaimed as Mrs. McGregor drove into town.

Violet laughed. "You're right, Benny. It smells like a bakery in here."

Mrs. McGregor parked the car by the curb across the street from the library. Henry carried the apple pie and Jessie took the lemon cake.

Balloons were everywhere. They were tied to the tables and the street lamps and to the backs of chairs. Colorful streamers hung from the library windows and rippled in the wind. On one side of the lawn, a man with a beard played a guitar while children sang along. A storyteller in a long dress sat in a circle and used puppets to tell her tale.

"Hello!" Mrs. Skylar called. "I'm so glad you could come to the library fair."

"We wouldn't think of missing it," Mrs. McGregor said.

"Mrs. McGregor made this cake and the pie," Jessie explained. "They're for the bake sale table."

"They look beautiful!" Mrs. Skylar exclaimed. "I'm sure we'll get a very large donation for them."

Mrs. McGregor beamed.

"Do you think this is a big enough donation for Mrs. McGregor's lemon cake?" Benny pulled a fist from his pocket. He opened his hand to show three nickels, a dime, two quarters, a rubber band, a gum wrapper, and a small rock.

Mrs. McGregor laughed. "Oh, Benny,"

she said. "I can make another lemon cake for you at home."

Henry plucked the rock and the gum wrapper from Benny's hand. He chuckled. "I don't think these are worth very much, Benny," he said.

"The rock does have pretty colors in it, though." Violet smiled at her little brother.

"Why don't we take the pie and the cake over to the bake-sale table for Mrs. McGregor," Jessie suggested. "Maybe you can buy some cookies or a cupcake with your coins."

"Okay. Let's go!" Benny darted off through the crowd.

"Benny! Wait for us!" Henry called. But it was too late. Thinking only of cookies, Benny had run far ahead.

Henry, Jessie, and Violet said goodbye to Mrs. McGregor and thanked her for the ride to the library fair. Then they headed toward the bake sale. They set Mrs. McGregor's pie and cake on the table.

"Where's Benny?" asked Jessie.

"I don't know," Henry replied. "I thought for sure we would see him here picking out some cookies."

"Excuse me," Violet said to the lady behind the table. "Was there a six-year-old boy with dark-brown hair here a few moments ago?"

"The table has been crowded," the lady said. "I'm not sure. Is that him over there?" She pointed through the crowd.

Violet ran toward the little boy, but it was not Benny.

Henry and Jessie looked worried.

"Maybe he couldn't find the bake-sale table," Violet said. "He's probably wandering nearby."

"Let's split up," Henry said. "We'll each go a different way and meet back here in ten minutes."

"Benny! Benny!" Henry, Jessie, and Violet ran through the crowd calling their brother's name. But he was nowhere in sight.

CHAPTER 5

A Vial of Blood?

Jessie found Benny walking down the sidewalk. There was a scrape on his knee and a trickle of blood running down his leg.

"Benny!" she cried, "Where have you been? We were so worried. What happened to your leg?"

Just then, Henry and Violet came running up to them.

Jessie settled Benny on a soft patch of grass under a tree. Violet ran to borrow the first-aid kit from Mrs. Skylar.

"Are you okay?" Henry asked.

Benny nodded bravely. He was almost as breathless as Violet when she returned with the first-aid kit.

Jessie cleaned the blood from his knee and squirted a bit of antiseptic on his cut. She covered it up with a bandage.

"I was running to the bake-sale table," Benny said. "I guess I wasn't watching where I was going. I crashed smack into a man and I fell to the ground."

"Is that how you hurt your knee?" Violet asked.

Benny nodded. "The man leaned down to help me up. I was so surprised. It was Mr. Hudson!"

"Mr. Hudson?" Henry said. "But he's away on his business trip. Are you sure it was him?"

Benny scratched his head. "Now I'm not so sure. I thought so at first. I called him Mr. Hudson when I apologized. When I said that name, he looked upset. He turned and left really fast."

"But where have you been?" asked Jessie.

"We looked all over for you."

"I followed him," Benny said.

"Benny! You shouldn't have done that. You should have stayed here by the library," Jessie said.

"I know. I'm sorry, Jessie. But the man dropped something. I tried to catch up with him so I could give it back. I didn't go far."

"Did you catch him?" asked Violet.

"No. He had an old blue bike down the street behind a tree. He rode away."

"What did he drop?" asked Henry.

Benny held out his hand. "This," he said.

Henry took the small plastic bottle from his brother. It was filled with a red liquid.

"What do you think it could be?" Jessie asked.

"I don't know," said Henry.

"I do," said Violet, putting her hand to her mouth. "It looks like…like…blood!"

The Alden children stared at each other for a few seconds. "I know it looks like blood," Henry said. "But it is probably something else. It could be ink."

"Or medicine," Jessie added. "Remember your cough syrup from last winter, Violet? It was red."

"I suppose that's true," Violet said. "But that is an odd bottle for cough medicine."

Henry put the bottle in his pocket. "I'll hold onto it in case we see the man again."

"Let's go to the diner," Jessie said. "I think we could all use a cool drink and some time to think."

"And some food!" Benny added.

It was lunch time, and the diner was very crowded. Nancy, a thin waitress with short blond hair, showed the Aldens to a booth in the back.

"How's this kids?" she asked.

"It's perfect. Thank you," said Jessie.

After they had placed their order, Jessie pulled out her notebook and a pencil. When facing a mystery, the Aldens often found that writing all the facts and clues on paper helped them to see what was going on.

Jessie wrote "Vampire Legend" at the top of the page. "What do we know about the

vampire legend?" she asked.

Henry took a long drink of his lemonade. "People around Greenfield used to tell stories about a vampire. We know that vampires are not real, so the people must have done it for fun or to scare each other."

"And Mr. Hudson heard those stories when he was growing up. He turned them into a book," Violet added.

"Then Mr. Hudson saw a vampire in the cemetery behind his house." Benny leaned across the table, his eyes wide.

"No, Benny. He saw something that concerned him. He didn't actually see a vampire," Henry said.

"Then what did he see?" asked Benny.

"We're not sure," Henry said.

Nancy stopped at the table with an armful of plates. "Here you go, kids," she said, setting down the plates of burgers and sandwiches.

Violet chewed thoughtfully on her grilled cheese. "One thing we do know," she said. "Mr. Hudson is trying to sell his house, but strange things are happening there that keep buyers away."

Jessie made a list. "There was the 'vampire' in the cemetery," she said. "And the broken flowerpots on the front porch."

"And someone keeps stealing the 'For Sale' sign." Violet finished her sandwich and placed her napkin on her plate.

"But why would anyone care if Mr. Hudson sold his house?" asked Benny.

"Mrs. Fairfax does not want him to move," Jessie said.

"That's true," Henry replied. "Do you think she could be the one behind all the strange happenings?"

Benny suddenly sat up very straight. "It's him," he whispered. "The man from the library."

"Where?" asked Henry who was across the table from Benny and facing the opposite direction.

"He's at the other end of the diner, sitting at the counter. I could give him back his bottle of blood...I mean, red stuff." Benny slid out of the booth. "Hurry, Henry. Give it to me. He's just about to leave."

Henry reached into his pocket, but it was too late. The man quickly jumped off his stool, his head lowered into his shirt, and darted out of the diner.

A few minutes later, Nancy stopped at the table to clear the plates. "Would you like to order dessert?" she asked.

"No, thank you," Jessie answered. "Not today."

"Excuse me," Henry asked. "Did you happen to wait on the man who was at the end of the counter? The one who left a few minutes ago?"

Nancy looked toward the empty stool. "Yes, I did," she answered. "Why do you want to know?"

"We have something of his," Henry said. "He dropped it earlier today and we wanted to give it back. Do you know where we can find him?"

"No," Nancy replied. "I'm sorry. I never saw him before. But it's odd that you say that. I have something for him too. He left the diner so quickly that he forgot to take his book with him."

"His book?" asked Violet.

"Yes." Nancy reached into the deep pocket of her apron. "It's a library book. He left it on the counter beside his plate."

She set the book on the table.

Jessie gasped. "*The Legend of the Vampire*!"

Benny pulled the book toward him and stared down at the blood red fangs of the man on the cover. "We could take it back to the library for you," he offered.

"Why, thanks," said Nancy. "I appreciate that. It will save me a trip. If the man comes back, I'll tell him that his book is at the library. Have a good day, kids."

When Nancy had left, Benny leaned across the table. "It's not *his* book. It's mine!"

CHAPTER 6

Accused

The Aldens walked slowly to Mr. Hudson's house on Whittaker Street.

"I don't understand why he would take Benny's book," Jessie said.

"Maybe it was an accident," Violet offered. "Maybe the book dropped out of Benny's bag and the man found it."

The children had no more time to talk. As they turned the corner onto Whittaker Street, they saw police cars in front of Mr. Hudson's house!

"There they are! They're the ones who did it!" Mrs. Fairfax stood on the sidewalk pointing at the Aldens.

The police turned to look at the children. A tall officer with black hair held a pad and a pen. "Excuse me, but who are you?" he asked

"We're the Aldens," Henry said. He introduced himself and his sisters and brother. "Is something wrong, Officer?"

Officer Franklin wrote their names on his pad. Then he looked up. "Someone vandalized this house last night."

"Oh, my!" Violet cried. A number of Mr. Hudson's beautiful flowers had been ripped from the ground and were lying across the walkway.

Benny was the first to see the words written across the porch boards in bright red letters. "'Leave…me…to…rest…in…pea…pea…'" He turned to Henry for help.

"'Leave me to rest in peace,'" Henry read. "'Or you will be sorry.'"

"It was those children who did it!" Mrs. Fairfax said. "I saw them here last night.

They were right there on the porch."

Officer Franklin looked at Henry. "Were you here last night?" he asked.

"Yes, officer," Henry replied. "But we sure didn't do this."

"Then what were you doing here?" the officer asked.

Just then the front door of Mr. Hudson's house opened. Josh rushed out.

"Thank goodness you children are here!" he said.

"You know them?" Officer Franklin asked Josh.

"Of course!" Josh replied. "These are the Aldens. Mr. Hudson told me that they would be stopping by today."

"And you don't suspect that they could have caused this damage?" the officer asked.

"What? No! Of course not. Mr. Hudson trusts them and so do I. He asked them to look after his place while he was away."

"Sorry, children," Officer Franklin said. "I hope you understand that it is my job to ask questions."

"We understand," Henry said.

Mrs. Fairfax banged her cane against the ground. "Seems to me you don't ask enough questions!" she said. "This used to be a nice, quiet street until that realtor and those children started coming around. They're up to something. You need to investigate them!" She stomped back to her house.

Josh ran his hands through his hair. "What am I going to do?" he asked. "The Bensons will be here in a few hours to look at the house. When they see this, they will never want to buy it."

"We'll clean it up," Jessie said. "We'll start right away."

"No," Josh said. "We can't clean it up. It is evidence. The police might need it. We should leave everything just the way it is."

Officer Franklin overheard them. "It's okay for you children to clean up the mess," he said. "We have taken pictures of everything. That is all we need."

Josh bit down on his lower lip and kicked at one of the upturned plants. "Are you sure?"

he asked. "We want you to find the person who did this."

"I'm sure," Officer Franklin replied. "We have all the information that we need."

The police officers left and Josh dropped onto the porch steps. "This is too much," he said.

"What do you mean?" asked Henry.

"Don't you see?" Josh asked. "It's the vampire!"

"But there's no such thing," Jessie said.

Josh's face was white. "It's right from the book," he said. "I've read it."

"*The Legend of the Vampire*?" asked Benny.

"Yes," Josh answered. "In the book, a vampire has his coffin hidden in the basement of an old home. A lonely old man lives by himself in the house. There is a cemetery behind the house. The vampire only comes out at night when the old man is sleeping. But one day the old man decides to sell the house. The vampire does not want his peace disturbed. He bites the neck of anyone who comes to live in the house."

Violet shivered. "What a terrible story!"

"What happens in the end?" Benny asked.

"No one will live in the house," Josh said. "The vampire has it all to himself." Josh looked over his shoulder and lowered his voice. "And the vampire still roams the cemetery every night!"

Jessie put her arm around Benny. "But it's just a story!" she said. "Everyone knows that vampires are not real."

Josh looked down. "I guess you're right, Jessie," he said. He grabbed an uprooted plant that was sitting on the step and tossed it angrily onto the lawn.

Violet picked it up.

"We should get to work," Henry said. "I need to cut the lawn."

"I'll replace the flowers the best that I can," Violet promised.

Jessie stared at the red letters on the porch. "I'll take care of cleaning that."

"What about me?" asked Benny.

Henry put his hand on Benny's shoulder. "Come with me, Benny," he said. "You can rake up the grass as I cut it."

"And I've got to make some phone calls." Josh stood and pulled a cell phone from his pocket. He pointed to the front lawn. "Can you believe that someone stole the 'For Sale' sign again? I'm running out of signs. I'm not sure that I even have any left."

The Aldens walked around to the shed to find the tools they needed. After the bright sunshine, the shed seemed very dark.

"Ouch!" Henry cried.

"Are you okay?" asked Jessie.

"Yes… I just stubbed my toe on the bike," Henry said.

"I don't remember the bike being in that spot yesterday," Violet said.

Henry wheeled the bike to the corner. "You're right, Violet. I think it was on the other side of the shed yesterday. That's odd."

Violet felt something fall down her neck. She cried out.

"What is it, Violet?" asked Jessie. "Are you okay?"

Violet laughed. "Yes," she said. "I guess I'm

a little jumpy. It's the chain for the light bulb. I must have backed into it. It tickled the back of my neck." Violet pulled the chain several times. It clicked, but nothing happened.

"The bulb must be out," said Henry.

"It's okay," Violet replied. "I've found the trowel and some gardening gloves. That's all I need. I'm going to go put those plants back in the ground right away. I don't want the roots to dry out and die. I know how proud Mr. Hudson is of his flowers."

There was a crash against the side of the shed. "I've found the rake!" Benny cried. "I'm all ready to help you, Henry."

Violet carried her tools to the front yard. She decided to work on the plants closest to the porch first. She knelt down and began to dig. She could hear Josh talking on his cell phone inside the house. His voice got louder as he came closer to the screen door on the porch.

"Yes," Josh said. "Mr. Hudson will have to lower the price now. Who will want to buy a house that has a vampire in the backyard?"

Then he laughed. "No," he said. "I don't really believe in vampires. But this is working out very well for us. When Mr. Hudson comes back from his trip, I will convince him that he should offer his house for much less money. Then you can buy it."

Violet stood up. What was Josh talking about?

"Violet!" Josh said. He quickly flipped his cell phone closed. "I didn't see you there! He walked out onto the porch.

"I'm sorry," Violet said. "I didn't mean to startle you. I was replanting the flowers."

Josh stuck his hands deep into his pockets. He looked around the corner of the house. "Are the others still out back?" he asked.

"Yes," Violet said.

"You shouldn't sneak around like that," Josh said. "Especially not with all the things that are going on around here."

"I wasn't sneaking," Violet tried to explain, but Josh's cell phone buzzed.

He looked at the number on the screen, but he did not answer it. He rubbed his stomach instead. "I am so hungry," he said. "I think I will walk over to the diner for a sandwich."

Henry pushed the lawn mower to the front yard. Benny pulled the rake behind him.

"This is going to be fun!" Benny said. "I wish there was a yard full of leaves for me to rake. Then I could make a big pile and jump in it."

"You'll have to wait a few weeks for the leaves to fall," Henry said.

"I'm going to ask Mr. Hudson if I can come back then and rake for him," Benny said.

Henry smiled. "I'm sure he would like that. But maybe he will have sold his house by then."

Violet was about to tell Henry about the person Josh had been speaking to on his cell phone. But just then Henry pulled the cord on the lawn mower. It roared to life.

"Sorry for the noise, Violet!" Henry shouted. "I will try to stay away from the flowers!"

Jessie had gone into the house and found a bucket and a scrub brush. A bottle of cleaner was under the kitchen sink. She filled the bucket with hot soapy water. Then she set to work trying to clean the red words from the porch.

Violet carefully placed the flowers back into the garden. Some of their stems were broken. It made her sad. She smoothed the loose dirt around each plant. Then she found a watering can in the shed and gave each plant a drink. She worked so hard that she forgot all about the conversation that she had overheard.

Mrs. Fairfax came out on her front porch every once in a while. She watched the Aldens with a wary look on her face. But the children were careful not to make too much noise and to stay off Mrs. Fairfax's property.

"There," Henry said, brushing loose grass from his jeans. "I think the house looks fine now."

"I don't know, Henry." Jessie shook her head. "The lawn looks nice and the flowers are beautiful. But I could not wash the letters off completely. If you look closely, you can still read what it says."

Henry walked up the steps to the porch. "I see what you mean. The porch might need to be repainted."

"We could never do that in time. The buyers will be here soon." Jessie sighed.

"I know what we can do!" Benny flung the door open and ran into the house. He returned a minute later. "How about this?" he asked. He held up a small rug.

"Great thinking, Benny!" Henry said.

"I remembered that it was in the kitchen by the sink," Benny said. "It will look nice out here, too."

Jessie took the rug and spread it in front of the porch door. "It doesn't cover everything," she said. "But it is a big improvement. Way to go, Benny."

Jessie locked the door and put the key back under the pot in the shed. Henry tied the bag of grass clippings and walked it to the curb.

"Isn't this Josh's car?" Henry asked.

"Yes," Violet answered. "Josh hasn't left yet. He walked to the diner for a sandwich about a half an hour ago."

"What's that in the back seat?" asked Benny.

The windows were up, but the Aldens could see something large in the back of Josh's car. Most of it was covered with a blanket. But two black metal stakes poked out from beneath the covering.

"It looks like a 'For Sale' sign is under that blanket," Jessie said.

The Aldens were puzzled.

"I thought Josh said he didn't have any more signs left," said Henry.

"It could be for a different house," Violet said. "I'm sure Josh has more than one house to sell. Or maybe it is a 'For Rent' sign for an apartment."

"You could be right, Violet," said Jessie.

Just then Josh came hurrying up the street. "What are you kids doing?" he called crossly. Josh quickly stood in front of his car with his hands on his hips.

"We're only putting the trash bag to the curb," Benny said. "Look at the lawn. Don't you think it looks good? I raked it!"

Josh's face relaxed. "Yes, Benny," he said. "Everything looks very nice again. Thank you. The Bensons should be here soon."

Jessie decided not to tell Josh about the red letters that did not wash off the porch. He still seemed too upset. He leaned back against his car and crossed his arms. His foot tapped nervously against the curb. And maybe Josh and the Bensons would not notice the few faint words that were not covered up by the rug.

The Aldens said goodbye to Josh and headed home.

CHAPTER 7

Three Suspects

Grandfather arrived for dinner just as Mrs. McGregor was setting a pot roast on the table.

"Smells great!" Grandfather said. "I'm sorry I'm late. My meeting lasted longer than I had thought."

Just then, there was a loud clap of thunder, and the lights flickered off and on for a minute. Rain drummed against the side of the house. The children quickly closed all the windows.

"You got home just in time, Grandfather."
Violet spread her napkin on her lap. "One
moment later and you would have been
caught in the storm."

"That's true. My timing was perfect."
Grandfather smiled. "I'm glad my
grandchildren are not out in this storm."

During dinner, the children told Grandfather about the vandalism at Mr. Hudson's
home and the work that they had done to
clean it up.

"That was very kind of you," Grandfather
said. "I wonder who would do such a thing?"

"We've been wondering the same thing,
Grandfather," said Henry.

Jessie spooned some warm applesauce
onto Benny's plate. "We think that whoever
it is does not want Mr. Hudson to sell his
house."

Violet was thinking hard. She'd heard Josh
on the phone the day before. She knew he
had said something about selling the house.
But she couldn't remember what he'd said.

Grandfather shook his head. "I suppose

the vandalism is why Mr. Hudson cut short his business trip."

"Mr. Hudson is home?" asked Henry.

"I thought so." Grandfather passed the mashed potatoes to Benny. "But I could be wrong. Driving home this evening, I thought I saw Mr. Hudson walking down the street near the library. I called out to him, but he turned a corner and disappeared."

After dinner, Grandfather went into his study to make some phone calls. Mrs. McGregor brought out an iced lemon cake and four plates.

"You brought home the lemon cake from the bake sale?" Benny clapped his hands.

"No, Benny," Mrs. McGregor replied. "Someone bought that cake and donated twenty dollars to the library for it."

"Twenty dollars! That must have been the biggest donation at the bake sale!" Violet smiled at Mrs. McGregor.

Mrs. McGregor's face flushed red with pride. "I don't know about that," she said.

"I don't think twenty dollars is enough."

Benny held out his empty plate. "I would pay one hundred dollars for your lemon cake!"

"That's why I made another one for you when I came home." Mrs. McGregor laughed. "And I'll even waive the hundred-dollar fee!"

The Aldens each ate a big slice of the good cake.

"Do you think the man that Grandfather saw today was Mr. Hudson?" asked Violet.

"I don't know," Henry said. "If it was Mr. Hudson, why didn't he say hello when Grandfather called out to him?"

"Maybe he didn't hear Grandfather," said Jessie.

"I thought I saw Mr. Hudson, too," said Benny. "But now I know it wasn't him."

"How do you know?" Jessie refilled Benny's glass with milk.

"The man I saw did not dress like Mr. Hudson. His clothes were old and not very clean. There was dirt on them and even some stains that looked like oil."

Violet tapped her fork on the table,

thinking. "You're probably right, Benny. Mr. Hudson seems to be a very neat person. I don't think he would wear dirty clothes."

Benny took a big gulp of milk. "He did look like Mr. Hudson, but it was probably just his white hair and mustache that confused me."

"I wonder if the Bensons showed up to look at the house this afternoon," Jessie said.

Benny wiped away his milk mustache. "I hope that Josh didn't say anything about vampires to them."

"Josh wouldn't do that," Henry said. "Not if he wants to sell the house for Mr. Hudson. Doesn't he want everyone to be interested in buying it?"

This reminded Violet of something. Something important. Suddenly she remembered what Josh had said on the phone. "Maybe he doesn't!" Violet said.

Henry, Jessie, and Benny looked very surprised.

"Why not, Violet?" asked Jessie. "Selling the house is Josh's job."

At last Violet told the others about the

conversation she had overheard. "He told the person on the phone that everything was working out well. When Mr. Hudson came back from his trip, Josh would convince him to lower the price for the house."

"That is very suspicious," Henry admitted.

Jessie crossed her arms. "And Josh did act strange when he noticed us standing next to his car."

"He knows all about the legend of the vampire," Benny added. "Remember how he told us the whole story?"

"Maybe Josh is behind the vandalism," Henry said. "He could be using scenes from the book to scare people away. If no one wants to buy the house, Mr. Hudson will have to offer it for a very low price."

Violet nodded. "And the person who Josh was speaking to on the phone would get a great house for not much money. That would be so unfair!"

"Maybe if we read Mr. Hudson's book, we can find more clues to this mystery," Henry said. "We might be able to find out what Josh will be up to next."

"If it *is* Josh, that is," Jessie added. "But what if it's Mrs. Fairfax? She doesn't want the house sold either. And since she lives next door, it would be easy for her to cause the damage and sneak back home."

"That's true." Violet folded her napkin. "And Mrs. Fairfax always hears us when we are at Mr. Hudson's house. Don't you think she would have heard the person who broke the flowerpots and wrote on the porch?"

"There is another suspect as well," Henry said. "We shouldn't forget about the man who ran into Benny at the library fair."

"But what could he have to do with it?" asked Benny.

Henry looked thoughtful. "I don't really know. But it is suspicious that he ran away from you when you called him by Mr. Hudson's name. And don't forget that he had your library book. He must have taken it from your backpack at Mr. Hudson's while we were inside having lunch."

"The book! It's gone again! I can't believe

it!" Benny slapped the side of his head.

"What's wrong?" asked Jessie.

"I left it on the kitchen table at Mr. Hudson's house. I set it down there so I could pull up the rug to use to cover the words written on the front porch. Afterwards, I forgot to go back inside for the book."

Henry laughed. "I think there is something mysterious about that book. It never stays in the same place."

"Can we go get it?" asked Benny.

"I suppose we can," said Henry. "But it will be dark soon. We can't ride our bikes."

Violet looked out the window. "The rain seems to have stopped."

The children cleaned up their dessert plates and put the cake away. They each found a flashlight to take on their nighttime walk. The air was slightly cool and the storm clouds were moving away. A round, full moon shone over Greenfield.

CHAPTER 8

Intruder

"What's that?" Violet asked as the children walked up Whittaker Street. "Did you see that light in Mr. Hudson's house?

The others had not seen it. "Maybe it was the moon shining on the window glass," Jessie suggested.

Violet was not so sure. But now the light was gone.

The rain had made the ground wet and muddy. The children's shoes squished in the lawn as they made their way toward the shed to retrieve the key to the house.

They each flicked on their flashlights. Jessie shone her beam on the shed door. Henry lifted the latch and the door squeaked open. The four Aldens stepped into the dark shed.

"Careful," Jessie warned. "Don't trip over the bicycle again."

"That's odd." Henry pointed his flashlight at the bike. "Didn't we move the bike to the left side of the shed today?"

"We did," Jessie agreed.

"Well, now it is on the right side of the shed."

Benny stood beside the bike. "And it's wet!" He shone his flashlight on the roof above the bike. "Even though there aren't any leaks in the roof."

"Someone has been riding this bike." Henry ran his hand over the dripping handlebars.

Violet walked over to look at the bike, but stumbled over an old suitcase. "What is this doing in the middle of the floor?"

"A suitcase?" Benny grabbed the handle

and moved the suitcase against the wall. It was heavy. "Wouldn't Mr. Hudson have taken his suitcase with him when he went on his trip?"

"It looks old," Henry said. "Maybe Mr. Hudson has a newer one that he uses."

Jessie shone her light on the flowerpot. She lifted it up. "It's gone!" she cried. "The key is not here. I know I put it right back under this pot before we left this afternoon."

"Are you sure?" Henry felt around on a lower shelf. "Maybe it fell down here."

Violet and Benny searched the floor.

"I'm positive," Jessie said. "Someone has taken it!"

The Aldens hurried from the shed. They quickly shut and latched the door and ran to the front of the house.

"Look at this!" Benny did not even need his flashlight. In the light of the moon, the children could clearly see a set of muddy footprints leading right up to Mr. Hudson's front door!

Henry put his hand carefully on the doorknob and turned. It was not locked. He entered the house. "Hello! Mr. Hudson! Are you home?" Henry turned to the others. "There's no one here."

"Let's get Benny's book and get home," Violet said.

Jessie flipped the light switch, but nothing happened. "The lights are out!"

"It's probably the circuit breaker," Henry said. "Sometimes a storm can shut it off, especially in an old house like this. I know where the switch is. Mr. Hudson pointed it out when he was showing me around the house. I might be able to get the lights back on."

Henry and Jessie carefully walked down the stairs into the basement. Violet and Benny waited by the front door.

"Did you hear that?" Violet asked, looking over her shoulder.

Benny cocked his head. "Yes. It sounds like footsteps. Do you think it could be Henry and Jessie?"

"No," Violet whispered. "I think it is

coming from outside. I wish Henry and Jessie would hurry up."

"You don't think it could be the vampire, do you?" asked Benny.

"There's no such thing," Violet said, but her voice was shaking. She turned and shut the front door, quickly turning the bolt.

A shaft of moonlight was shining through the window and it fell across the carpeted floor. The rest of the house was dark. As Violet and Benny watched, a dark shadow flitted slowly across the moonlit carpet.

"What was that?" asked Benny, grabbing Violet's hand.

"I'm not sure," Violet answered. "Maybe it was a cloud passing in front of the moon."

"But it was shaped like a bat!" Benny cried.

Violet didn't want to frighten Benny, but she knew he was right. A large bat had just slowly passed by the window.

Suddenly the lights flashed on. Henry and Jessie pounded up the basement stairs.

"It was only the switch, just as I thought," Henry said, coming through the door. He stopped in his tracks when he saw the kitchen. Sitting on the table was a glass of milk and a plate with a half-eaten sandwich. Next to them was Benny's library book, *The Legend of the Vampire*, open to page 136.

Violet gasped. "Someone was here!"

"You're right, Violet." Henry walked to the table. "And whoever it was left in a hurry. This glass of milk is still cold."

"And here is the missing key!" Jessie picked up the key from the kitchen counter.

"I think we should go," Violet said.

Henry agreed. "We need to let Mr. Hudson know that someone has been inside his house."

"And it wasn't a vampire," Benny said, nodding at Violet, "because vampires don't eat sandwiches." He picked up his library book and stared at the front cover. "They only like blood!"

"Benny and I heard footsteps outside while you were in the basement," Violet explained. "We need to be very careful."

The children stepped outside and peered

up and down the street. Jessie locked the door
tightly and put the key into her pocket. She
left the porch light on. The children hurried
home as fast as they could.

CHAPTER 9

A Mysterious Photo

Later that night the Aldens sat in the living room each with a mug of hot chocolate and plate of cookies. Henry opened *The Legend of the Vampire* to Chapter One. He began to read.

The cemetery on Whittaker Street was dark and cold. Martha stood by the gate and pulled her coat close around her body. She wrapped her scarf tightly around her neck. A chill ran down her spine, and she turned just in time to see a strange man in a long, dark cape gliding toward her neighbor's quaint little house. At first she had hoped that it was Francis, coming home after all these years. But when she saw the pale, white skin, the blood red lips, and the piercing black eyes of the stranger, she knew that it was not Francis. Those eyes held her for a moment and as they did, Martha felt the blood pounding through her veins. Was it fear or excitement that made her heart flutter so violently? Just as suddenly as he arrived, the stranger disappeared into her neighbor's basement, so quickly that it seemed he simply melted himself through the walls.

"Oh my!" cried Mrs. McGregor standing in the doorway. "What a frightening book to be reading before bed. It would give me nightmares!"

Benny rubbed his eyes and yawned.

"We're looking for clues to a mystery in the story. Strange things are happening at Mr. Hudson's house."

"I've heard about it," Mrs. McGregor said. "Oh yes, and a man named Josh called a few minutes ago. He said Mr. Hudson is coming home tomorrow. It seems he didn't need to stay as long as he'd planned. Also, Josh said you left milk on the table and mud on the porch."

The children looked at each other.

"We'll go over there first thing in the morning." Jessie said.

Henry nodded. "We need to tell Mr. Hudson someone was in his house."

Mrs. McGregor held a bag of mini marshmallows in her hand. "Also, I thought you might like to have some of these in your hot chocolates. Goodnight, children."

They all thanked Mrs. McGregor and wished her a good night.

Jessie reached for the marshmallows and sprinkled a few on the top of her hot chocolate. "Josh must have been at

Mr. Hudson's house tonight."

"But why would he go over there so late?" wondered Violet.

Henry shrugged. "It does seem odd. I doubt he'd to show the house to a buyer late at night."

Benny dropped a few marshmallows into his mug and a whole handful into his mouth. "Maybe he was looking for the vampire."

Henry stood to take a cookie from the platter and *The Legend of the Vampire* fell to the floor. When he picked it up, he saw something sticking out from the pages. It was an old black-and-white photograph. The edges were a little crumpled, and a crease ran down one side.

"Look at this!"

Jessie, Violet, and Benny crowded around the photo in Henry's hand.

"That's Mr. Hudson's house!" Violet pointed to the home that was in the background of the photo.

"Who do you think those two boys are?" asked Benny.

Two young children were posed in front of the porch. One looked to be about Henry's age, fourteen, and the other one seemed to be a little younger than Benny. The younger boy had his hand resting on the seat of a shiny, new bicycle.

Violet gasped. She pointed to the older boy. "That must be Mr. Hudson."

"I'm sure you're right!" Jessie exclaimed. "And the other one must be his little brother."

Benny's fingers were sticky from the marshmallows, so he did not touch the photo. But he pointed at the two boys. "They sure do look an awful lot alike."

"Yes," Violet agreed. "If they were the same age, I would think they were twins."

"But how did the picture get in the book?" Benny wondered. "Do you think it was stuck in that book in the library for all those years?"

Henry turned the photo over in his hand. "No. I don't think it was in the book before today. See this crease mark? I think the photo was folded and carried in someone's wallet for a long time."

Henry pulled his wallet from his back pocket. He slid the picture in and out of the billfold. "See? When it is folded at the crease, this photo fits perfectly in a wallet. You wouldn't need to fold it if you were going to keep it in a book."

"That makes a lot of sense, Henry," Violet said.

"Look, there's some faded writing on the bottom." Jessie took the picture and held it up to the light. "It's hard to read."

Benny ran from the room and quickly returned with a magnifying glass that he had gotten as a gift on his last birthday. "This will help!" he cried.

"Thanks, Benny." Henry held the magnifying glass over the faded writing. It helped the children see the faded ink. Slowly, the Aldens puzzled out each letter.

"'Charles!'" Jessie exclaimed. "The first word is '"Charles!'"

"Mr. Hudson's first name is Charles," Violet remembered.

"A...n...d," Benny read. "'And!' I know that word."

Violet smiled. "Good job, Benny."

The last word was the most faded. Before long, though, the Aldens had spelled "F-r-a-n-c-i-s."

"Francis must be Mr. Hudson's younger brother," Jessie said.

Henry was paging through *The Legend of the Vampire*, checking to see if any more pictures could be stuck between its pages. He did not find any. He paused at the dedication page. "Look at this."

Jessie read aloud: "'This book is dedicated to my dear brother, Francis.'"

"We didn't even have to read the book to find clues in it!" Benny exclaimed.

Henry set the book back on the table with the picture carefully placed inside. "We'll have a lot to tell Mr. Hudson when we see him tomorrow morning."

CHAPTER 10

Caught!

The next morning, after a quick breakfast of cereal and fruit, the Aldens jumped on their bikes and quickly rode to Mr. Hudson's house. But there was a police car in front! It was just driving away as the children walked up the front steps.

Jessie knocked on the front door.

"Come on in, kids," Mr. Hudson called from the living room. He was sitting on the couch, his suitcase dumped on the floor beside the coffee table. His hair was uncombed and there were dark circles under his eyes.

Josh stood in the corner with his hands thrust deeply into his pockets.

"Is everything all right?" Jessie asked. "We just saw the police car."

"The police were here looking for finger-prints," Mr. Hudson said. "Someone has broken into my home!"

Josh stepped forward. "No locks or windows were broken," he said. He stared at the Aldens. "Someone must have left the door unlocked. And it wasn't me!"

Mr. Hudson looked at the children. "I don't blame you," he said. "I even forget to lock the door sometimes. I know you meant well."

"But we *did* lock the door!" Jessie insisted. "We are very responsible. The person who broke into your home knew where the key was hidden. He took it from the shed and let himself in. We found the key last night on the kitchen counter."

Mr. Hudson looked up sharply.

"You must have told some of your friends

where that key was," Josh said accusingly. "Who else could know where the key was hidden?"

"I can promise you that we did not tell anyone," Jessie answered.

Mr. Hudson ran his hands through his hair. "Someone was in the shed," he said. "My plane came in very early this morning. When I got home, I heard noises coming from the shed. I called the police right away. The person in the shed ran away through the cemetery when the police arrived. The officers chased him. I don't know if they caught him yet or not. Perhaps he found the key by accident and let himself in when I was away."

The Aldens looked at each other.

"Was the person who ran from the shed as tall as the vampire that you have been seeing in the cemetery lately?" asked Henry.

"What?" Mr. Hudson sat up very straight. "The vampire? Josh, have you been telling stories?"

"It's not just a story," Josh answered. "You

told me yourself that you saw something strange in the cemetery at night."

"I saw a person," Mr. Hudson explained to the children. "He dressed and acted like the vampire from my book, *The Legend of the Vampire*. Whenever I tried to call out to him or to catch him, he ran away."

"Do you think the person in the shed could have been the one who acted like the vampire?" Henry asked.

"I suppose so," Mr. Hudson answered. "He was about the same height. But who would want to do such a thing? I don't understand."

Jessie put her hand on Mr. Hudson's shoulder. "Mr. Hudson, was there anyone at all besides you who knew where you hid the spare key?"

Mr. Hudson was quiet for some time. "Besides you four children, there might be one other person," he said. "But it couldn't have been him."

The Aldens weren't so sure. "Mr. Hudson," Henry said. "We think it may have been your brother Francis who took the spare key and

let himself into your home."

"Francis? What? How do you know that name?" Mr. Hudson's eyes were wide with surprise.

Benny took the folded photo from the pages of the book and handed it to Mr. Hudson.

Mr. Hudson drew in his breath sharply. He cradled the photo gently in his hands. "Where did you get this?" he finally asked.

"We found it," Benny replied, "stuck between the pages of *The Legend of the Vampire*."

"This is a picture of my brother and me!" Mr. Hudson cried.

Just then there were heavy footsteps on the front porch. Two police officers opened the screen door and brought in a man in handcuffs. He was dirty and disheveled. He looked almost exactly like Mr. Hudson.

Mr. Hudson jumped to his feet. "Francis!" he cried. He threw his arms around his brother.

The officers looked confused.

"Please, officer," Mr. Hudson asked. "Take those handcuffs off. This has all been a big misunderstanding. This is my brother."

"You're not going to press charges?" asked the officer. "He has already admitted that he broke into your home."

"No, no, of course I'm not going to prosecute," Mr. Hudson said hurriedly. "There has been no crime here. My brother is welcome in this house at any time."

The officer shook his head disapprovingly, but he removed the cuffs. Mr. Hudson thanked the police for all their help and showed them to the door.

After Francis was comfortably seated in a chair with a glass of lemonade and a clean shirt borrowed from his brother, the Aldens explained what they knew.

"While you were away," Henry said, "Benny ran into a man at the library fair who looked exactly like you."

"I thought it was you at first, Mr. Hudson," Benny said. "But then I realized that the man was too..." Benny paused.

"Messy." Francis finished the sentence.

"Yes," Benny agreed, his face coloring. "Mr. Hudson is always dressed so neatly."

"We may look alike," Francis said, "but other than that we are as different as brothers can be."

"We are very different," Mr. Hudson agreed. "And I'm sorry to say that it led to quite a few fights when we were younger."

"I'm sorry about those fights, Charles," Francis said.

"I am, too." Mr. Hudson looked at the Aldens. "Francis and I loved each other, but we disagreed about many things."

"Charles was fussy and neat," Francis said. "His half of the room was always clean and organized. I was a lot a messier and I drove him crazy sometimes."

Mr. Hudson smiled. "And Francis was a great athlete, but I couldn't even run without tripping over my own two feet. Francis liked to go sleep early, especially before big games, while I liked to stay up late reading. He used to be so annoyed with me for keeping the light on."

Both brothers laughed at the memories.

"After our parents died, we fought a lot more often," Francis said.

"I wanted you to stay in school and get a good education," Mr. Hudson remembered.

Francis nodded. "And I wanted to quit school and work in my friend's carpentry shop. One day, after a particularly big fight, I got very angry and I left home without a word. Since then, I've traveled all around the country. I've lived and worked in many different states. My life has been very interesting. But throughout all those years, I always missed my home and my brother."

"Why didn't you call or write?" asked Mr. Hudson. "I always wondered where you were."

"I thought you might not want me back," Francis explained. "I know that I was quite a troublemaker. I was afraid that we would just start fighting again. Then, a few months ago, I finally decided to take the risk and come back and see you. The older I've gotten, the more I've realized how much my family and my old home mean to me. I was going to surprise you. But when I saw the sign on the lawn that said that the house was for sale, I became angry. You weren't ever supposed to sell this house, Charles. Our parents wanted us to keep it in the family as long as we were alive. But I had been gone for so long. I knew I couldn't demand anything from you."

"So you decided to scare away the people who came to buy the house?" Henry asked.

"Yes." Francis hung his head. "I admit it. I pretended to haunt the graveyard at night. I wore a cape and I even sprinkled fake blood on tombstones and people's back porches. I tried to do all the things that the vampire did in the stories you used to tell me when we were growing up. I knew it would start people talking and word would get around. I thought that no one would want to buy a house with a vampire in the backyard."

Henry pulled a small vial from his pocket. "Was this the blood that you used?"

"Yes!" Francis exclaimed. "But it is only

colored water. Where did you find that?"

"You dropped it when we bumped into each other at the library fair," Benny explained. "I tried to catch you to give it back, but you ran away."

"I was worried when you called me 'Mr. Hudson'," Francis said. "I thought you might know who I was. I didn't want Charles to know I was in town until I had finished scaring away all the buyers for the house."

"Did you take *The Legend of the Vampire* from my backpack?" asked Benny.

"I did," Francis said. "I saw you put it in there on that first day that you met my brother. I needed more ideas for my vampire haunting. I knew I could find them in the book."

"And then you left the picture in the book," Jessie added.

"Yes. I was so surprised to see young Benny there at the diner, that I jumped up and left, leaving the book behind. Imagine how surprised I was to find the book on the kitchen table later that night."

"That's because I left it there by accident."
Benny sighed.

"I figured as much," Francis said. "The
flowers were replanted and the porch was
scrubbed. I knew you kids had been here."

"You wrote those terrible words in ink
on our front porch?" Charles asked. "How
could you do that?"

Francis looked sheepish. "I'm very sorry,
Charles. I promise to repaint the porch for
you. I was only trying to be a good vampire.
But I suppose I didn't do a very good job of it.
The Aldens came back to the house at night.
I thought they would be too frightened for
that."

"We were looking for the book," Benny
explained.

"I knew Charles had gone out of town
and so I took the key from under the pot.
We always kept it there, even when we were
children. I was having a nice sandwich and
reading by flashlight when you children
surprised me. I rushed into the basement.
When I heard footsteps on the stairs I had

to quickly sneak out the back door. I circled around to the front. I thought I could get back in to get the rest of my sandwich and the book, but these two kids where standing by the door." Francis pointed at Violet and Benny.

"You tried to scare us with a bat," Benny said.

Francis chuckled. He put his two hands together and flapped his fingers as though they were wings. "Remember this, Charles? We used to make all kinds of animal shapes in the shadows at night. I was quite good at it."

"You still are!" Violet said. "It looked very much like a real bat. We were frightened."

Mr. Hudson shook his head. "Francis, I wish you hadn't done all these things. I wish you had just come and talked to me."

Francis sighed. "I know that now. And I'm sorry." Francis turned to Violet. "I apologize for frightening you."

"And where did you put all the 'For Sale' signs that you stole?" asked Mr. Hudson.

"You have to return them to Josh. You upset him as well."

Francis looked confused.

"Your brother didn't steal the 'For Sale' signs," Violet said. "Josh did that."

"What?" Mr. Hudson turned to look at his realtor. "Why would Josh steal his own signs? That doesn't make any sense. He wants to sell the house. It's his job."

Josh stuck his hands even deeper into his pockets. He seemed to be trying to find something to say.

"Josh has a friend who wants your house, Mr. Hudson," Violet explained. "Only he can't afford to buy it unless you lower the price. Josh didn't start the vampire rumors, but he helped them along. He thought that if buyers were frightened away, you would be happy to sell the house for a lot less money to his friend. I saw the missing 'For Sale' signs in the back of Josh's car and I overheard him on the phone with his friend."

Josh's face was bright red. "You should know that it is not right to eavesdrop!" he shouted at Violet.

"I was not eavesdropping!" Violet crossed her arms and stood her ground. "I was working in the garden when you made a call near the front porch. I couldn't help but hear what you said."

"And you should know that you were supposed to be working for me and not for your friend," Mr. Hudson added. "You're fired as my realtor, Josh."

Josh bit hard on his lower lip. He took a few steps toward the door, then turned back around. "I'm very sorry, Charles," he said. "And I'm sorry for accusing you, Violet. My friend doesn't have a lot of money and he has five children. I thought this would be the perfect house for him. But it was wrong of me to try to ruin your chances of selling at a good price. I didn't mean any harm, but I know what I did was wrong. I hope you'll forgive me."

Josh pushed open the screen door to leave just as Mrs. Fairfax was about to knock.

"What is going on over here?" she

complained, stepping into the living room. "All this commotion has got to stop. Realtors, children, police cars. What next?"

"Hello, Martha," said Francis.

"Francis? Is that Francis?" Mrs. Fairfax put her hand over her heart.

Mr. Hudson helped Mrs. Fairfax into a seat. "It's my brother all right, Martha," he said with a smile. "He's come back to live with me."

"So you're not selling the house?" Mrs. Fairfax asked.

Mr. Hudson looked at his brother and paused. "No, I'm not selling. That is," he continued, "as long as Francis agrees to move in and help me out with the house."

Francis stood and threw his arm around his brother's shoulder. "Thank you, Charles," he said. "There is nothing I would like better. It is so good to be home!"

Suddenly, a loud growling noise came from the sofa. Everyone turned to look.

Benny's face turned bright red. He clasped his hands over his stomach. "Excuse me," he apologized.

Everyone laughed, even Mrs. Fairfax.

"I suppose tracking down vampires can make a person quite hungry." Mr. Hudson smiled.

"*Everything* makes Benny hungry," Henry explained.

Mr. Hudson brought out a pitcher of lemonade and set a tray of snacks on the table for his company.

Everyone was excited when Mr. Hudson told them that the producers had agreed to film the movie version of *The Legend of the Vampire*. It was going to be set right in Greenfield.

"Maybe we can all have a role in the film!" Benny cried.

"That would be so exciting," Jessie agreed. "At the very least, perhaps we can come and watch the filming. Would that be all right with you, Mr. Hudson?"

"Of course!" Mr. Hudson said. "You are more than welcome."

"Are you going to write any more books,

Mr. Hudson?" Violet asked.

"I never stop writing, Violet," Mr. Hudson said. "And I'm always looking for ideas for my next story."

As Benny reached for a third helping of cheese and crackers, his stomach let out another loud growl.

Mr. Hudson laughed. "Maybe my next book could be called *The Legend of the Bottomless Stomach*."

"And if that book is made into a movie, I could have the lead role!" Benny grinned. "I knew my stomach would make me famous!"